AF207000

BODY PARTS

Izzi Howell

PowerKiDS press

Published in 2024 by The Rosen Publishing Group, Inc.
2544 Clinton Street, Buffalo, NY 14224

First published in Great Britain in 2017 by Wayland

Picture credits:

iStock: EcoPic 13bl, Squaredpixels 18, Antagain 21r; Shutterstock: elephant cover l, hand cover r, Sabphoto title page and 15t, Africa Studio 4, Nejron Photo 5t, Kuttelvaserova Stuchelova 5b, Halfbottle 6, wildestanimal 7t, hagit berkovich 7bl, Yevhenii Chulovskyi 7br, Blend Images 8, Andrew M. Allport 9t, bikeriderlondon 9b, In Green 10, Anneka 11t, Zoltan Major 11c, nattanan726 11b, Gelpi 12, clearviewstock 13t, FotoRequest 13br, Patrick Foto 14tl, all_about_people 14tr, David Alexander Stein 14b, Kletr 15b, photka and tratong 16-17t, john michael evan potter 16b, Giedriius 17bl, Anton_Ivanov 17br, Dejan Stanisavljevic 19tl, Coffeemill 19tr, anat chant 19bl, Anan Kaewkhammul 19br, Jorg Hackemann 20, nbiebach 21tl, Iakov Filimonov 21bl.

All design elements from Shutterstock.

Editor: Izzi Howell
Design: Clare Nicholas

The author, Izzi Howell, is a writer and editor
specializing in children's educational publishing.

Cataloging-in-Publication Data
Names: Howell, Izzi.
Title: Body parts / Izzi Howell.
Description: New York : Powerkids Press, 2024. | Series: Human body, animal bodies | Includes index.
Identifiers: ISBN 9781642828092 (pbk) | ISBN 9781642828108 (library bound) |
ISBN 9781642828115 (ebook)
Subjects: LCSH: Animal anatomy-- Juvenile literature | Biology--Classification--Juvenile literature |
Human anatomy--Juvenile literature
Classification: LCC OL806.5 H69 2024 | DDC 570--dc23

Manufactured in the United States of America

CPSIA Compliance Information: Batch #CSPK24. For further information contact Rosen Publishing at 1-800-237-9932.

Find us on

Contents

Human and animal bodies

Human bodies and animal bodies look different. However, we have some of the same body parts!

wing
a parrot
head
feather
Squawk!
foot
head
foot
toes
scales
tail
neck
a gecko
leg

Head

Humans have two eyes, a mouth, and a nose on their face. Our face is at the front of our head. We have ears on the sides of our head.

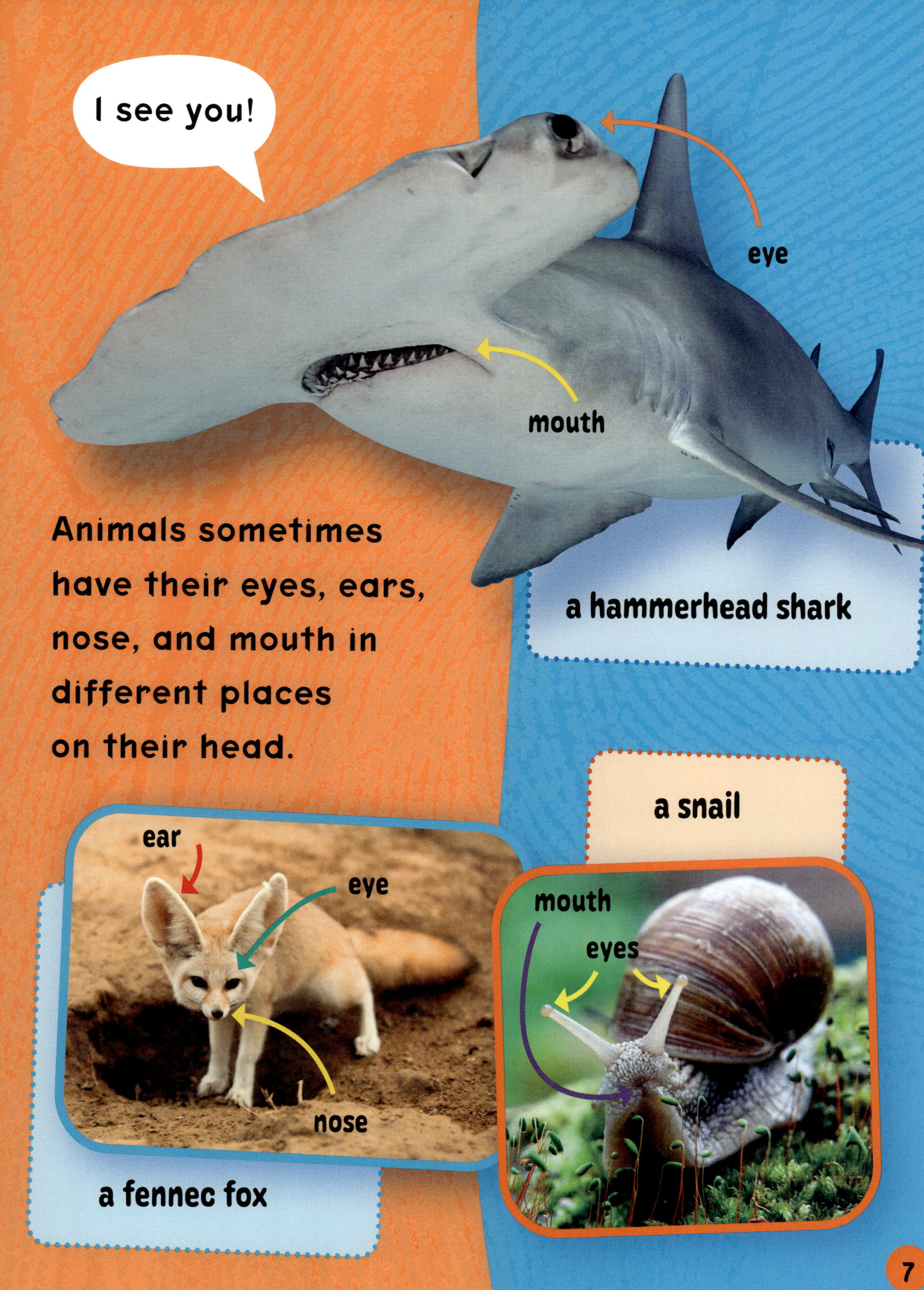

Animals sometimes have their eyes, ears, nose, and mouth in different places on their head.

Neck

Our neck allows us to turn and move our head. Humans can't move their head very far in any direction.

Owls can turn their head almost all the way around! They can't move their eyes like humans can, so they move their head instead.

Giraffes have very long necks. This helps them eat leaves from the tops of trees.

Skin

Skin protects our body. It stops germs from getting inside.

Animal skin looks and feels different than human skin.

moist tree frog skin

shiny red snapper scales

What do you think snake skin feels like?

hard crocodile scales

Hair and fur

Long, thick hair grows on human heads.
Short, fine hair grows all over our body.

a tiger

stripy fur in long grass

Some animals are covered in thick fur. The color of their fur helps them to hide in the wild.

white fur in snow

beige fur in sandy soil

a snowshoe hare

meerkats

Can you think of another animal with white fur?

Arms, wings, and fins

Humans can bend their arms at the elbow. We can move our arms **up**... **across**...

common egrets

and **out**.

Fish move their fins to change direction in the water. Their tail fin pushes them forward.

a clown fish

Birds have wings instead of arms. When most birds flap their wings, they fly up into the sky.

Hands

Inside human hands there are lots of tiny bones. They allow us to move our fingers in different ways.

an African elephant's trunk

a sea eagle's claws

a spider monkey's tail

Legs

Humans stand on two legs. We use our legs to walk, run, skip, and jump.

Some animals have two legs. Others have four, six, eight, or many more.

Feet

Our feet support the
weight of our body
when we are standing
up. Humans have five
toes on each foot.

Some animals have webbed feet. Others have paws and hooves.

a cat's paw

a duck's webbed foot

a Bactrian camel's hoof

Human and animal classification

Mammals

African
elephant

Bactrian
camel

cat

deer

fennec fox

giraffe

human

meerkat

snowshoe
hare

spider
monkey

tiger

FEATURES

two or four legs

fur or skin

Birds

common egret

duck

flamingo

owl

parrot

sea eagle

FEATURES

wings

two legs

feathers

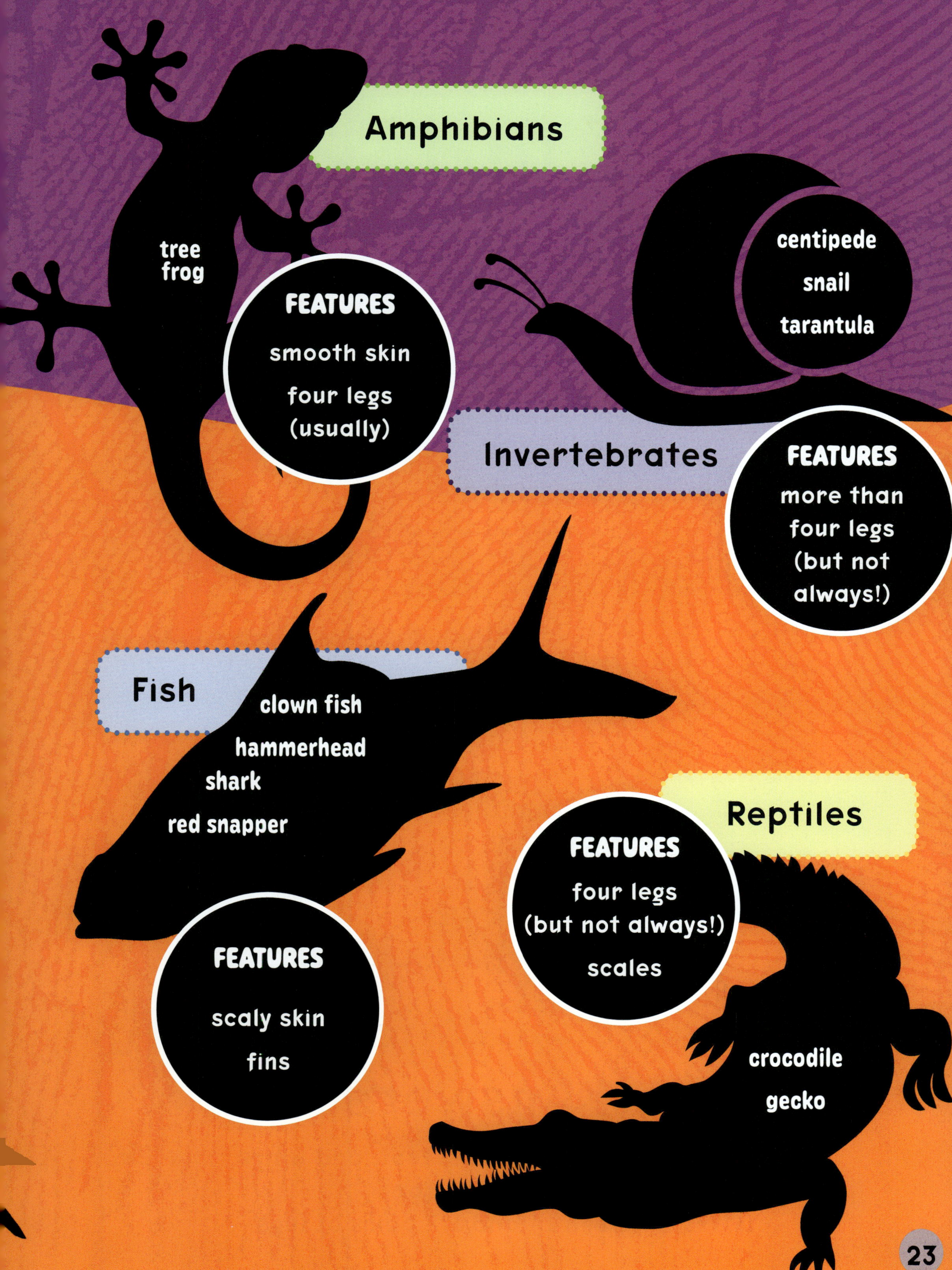

Amphibians
tree frog
FEATURES
smooth skin
four legs
(usually)
centipede
snail
tarantula
Invertebrates
FEATURES
more than
four legs
(but not
always!)
Fish
clown fish
hammerhead
shark
red snapper
FEATURES
scaly skin
fins
Reptiles
FEATURES
four legs
(but not always!)
scales
crocodile
gecko
23

Index

Answers

p4 – Arms, hands, legs, feet, and wings

p13 – Polar bear, arctic fox

p19 – Between 14 and 177 pairs of legs